D1401874

Fingers Aren't Food

Written by Payson Hendrix and Illustrated by Rich Hennemann

Fingers Aren't Food

First Edition

Story help from Brandon Hendrix

ISBN 978-0-578-50132-1

Distributed and Published by Little Storm Publishing

Little Strom Publishing
PO BOX 56
Hudson, MA 01749

Designed in Boston MA and manufactured in Boston

Learn More at LittleStormPublishing.com

For Callan

Hi! I'm Theo. We're going to the zoo.

I love the zoo!

Mom! Let's go! Please.

What's my favorite animal?

I can only pick one?
That seems silly.

Hmm. Let's see.

Monkeys are
funny.

They swing a lot.
I like to swing.

The macaws look like rainbows.

They yell at me sometimes.
My sister yells at me sometimes, too.

Their sign says:

PLEASE
DON'T
FEED
FINGERS
TO THE
BIRDS

This zoo is funny!
Fingers aren't food.

Do I like giraffes? Have you seen the neck on them?!

Someday I'll be that tall! I climb trees to reach high up leaves like the giraffe.

Did I scare you? The lemurs always look scared to see me. I make that face back at them and it makes me laugh!

Do I feed the deer?

Sometimes we walk through the deer forest.

These deer are not like the deer in my yard.
They like people.

What else would I feed a deer?

It's not like they would want to eat my fingers!
Fingers aren't food.

Coming!

Mom says it is time to go. I am so excited!

I still did not pick my favorite animal?
Hmm. Maybe the giant tortoise.
They eat a lot of salad.

They do not have a sign. They are smart. They know
Fingers aren't food.

Speaking of food...

**Mom? I am hungry!
Can we get lunch
at the zoo?**

Hooray! Thanks, Mom. What can I get?

SNACK BAR MENU

HAMBURGER	$3.99		CHIPS	$1.00
FRENCH FRIES	$1.99		CANDY	$1.25
CHICKEN FINGERS	$7.99		COOKIE	$1.00
PIZZA	$3.99			
HOT DOG	$2.99		SODA	$2.00
POPCORN	$1.99		WATER	$2.00
NACHOS	$4.99		JUICE	$1.50

POP CORN

WHAT??!!!

chicken